New Orleans

Hedlund, Stephanie F.
AR BL: 5.2
Points: 0.5   LG

BATTLE GROUND ACADEMY
Franklin, TN

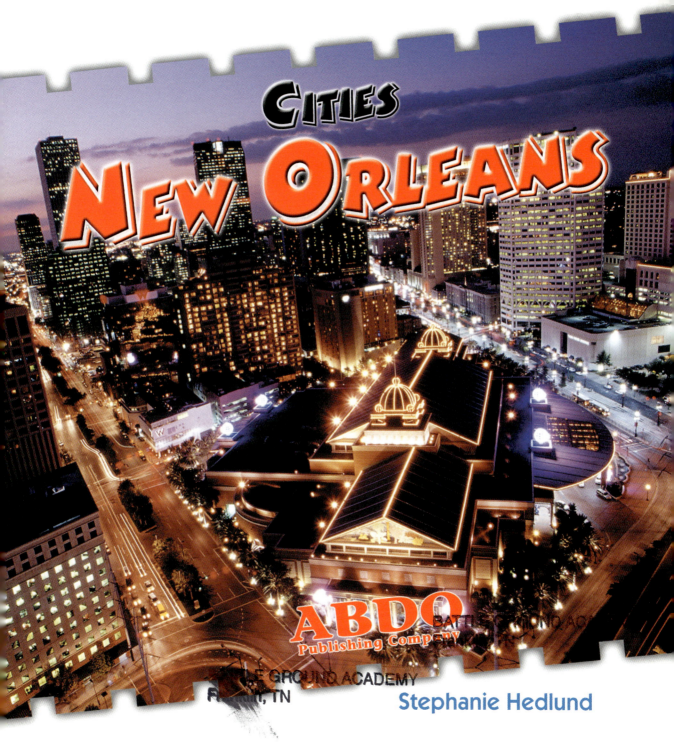

visit us at
www.abdopublishing.com

Published by ABDO Publishing Company, 4940 Viking Drive, Edina, Minnesota 55435. Copyright © 2007 by Abdo Consulting Group, Inc. International copyrights reserved in all countries. No part of this book may be reproduced in any form without written permission from the publisher. The Checkerboard Library™ is a trademark and logo of ABDO Publishing Company.

Printed in the United States.

Cover Photo: Corbis
Interior Photos: Corbis pp. 1, 5, 6-7, 13, 14, 15, 18, 19, 20, 21, 23, 24, 25, 26, 27, 28, 29;
    North Wind pp. 8, 9, 11

Series Coordinator: Megan Murphy
Editors: Rochelle Baltzer, Megan Murphy
Art Direction & Maps: Neil Klinepier

All U.S. population statistics are from the 2000 census taken by the U.S. Census Bureau.

Library of Congress Cataloging-in-Publication Data

Hedlund, Stephanie F., 1977-
    New Orleans / Stephanie Hedlund.
       p. cm. -- (Cities)
    Includes index.
    ISBN-10 1-59679-721-5
    ISBN-13 978-1-59679-721-5
    1. New Orleans (La.)--Juvenile literature. I. Title. II. Series.

F379.N5H43 2006
976.3'35--dc22

2005031725

CONTENTS

New Orleans 4
New Orleans at a Glance 6
Timeline 7
Early History 8
Construction 10
Steady Growth 12
Katrina 14
Surrounded 16
Mississippi 18
Election Day 20
New Orleanians 22
Things to See 26
Things to Do 28
Glossary 30
Saying It 31
Web Sites 31
Index 32

NEW ORLEANS

New Orleans is the largest city in Louisiana. It has a key location near the Gulf of Mexico, the Mississippi River, and Lake Pontchartrain. This location has made it one of the busiest ports in the world.

In the beginning, much of New Orleans was swampland. Some areas of the city are still six feet (2 m) below sea level. The city has continued to grow over the years. Today, it has an area of 181 square miles (469 sq km).

New Orleans has an interesting history and a special **culture**. Its citizens are a blend of French, Spanish, and other **ethnic** groups. This gives the city a distinctive atmosphere that isn't found anywhere else.

New Orleans has been a popular place for people to visit. In 2005, the city was hit by a hurricane. This natural disaster caused flooding in most of the city. Today, its citizens are working to make New Orleans a great place to visit again.

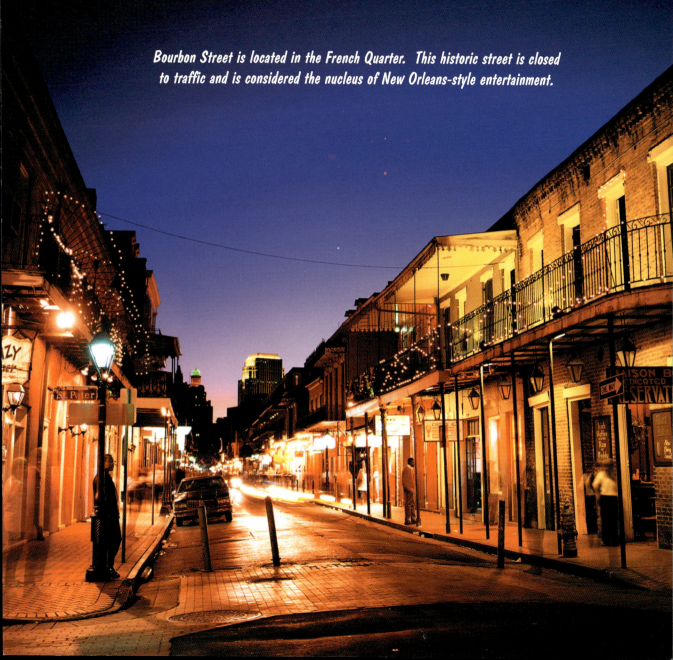

Bourbon Street is located in the French Quarter. This historic street is closed to traffic and is considered the nucleus of New Orleans-style entertainment.

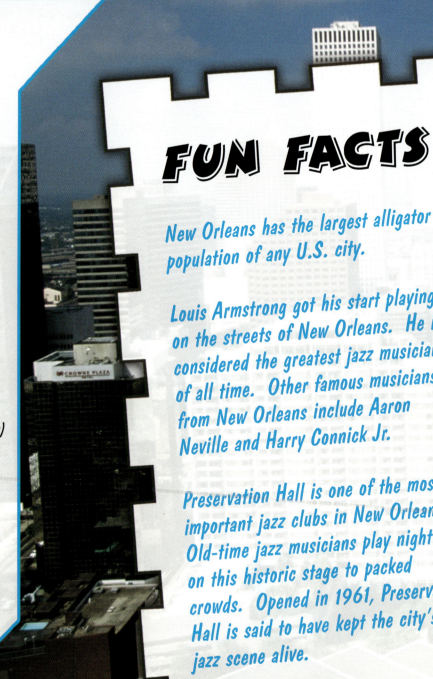

NEW ORLEANS AT A GLANCE

Date of Founding: 1718
Population: 484,674
Metro Area: 181 square miles (469 sq km)
Average Temperatures:
- 60° Fahrenheit (16 °C) in cold season
- 77° Fahrenheit (25 °C) in warm season

Annual Rainfall: 57 inches (145 cm)
Elevation: 2 feet (.6 m)
Landmarks: Mississippi River, Lake Pontchartrain, French Quarter
Money: U.S. dollar
Language: English

FUN FACTS

New Orleans has the largest alligator population of any U.S. city.

Louis Armstrong got his start playing on the streets of New Orleans. He is considered the greatest jazz musician of all time. Other famous musicians from New Orleans include Aaron Neville and Harry Connick Jr.

Preservation Hall is one of the most important jazz clubs in New Orleans. Old-time jazz musicians play nightly on this historic stage to packed crowds. Opened in 1961, Preservation Hall is said to have kept the city's jazz scene alive.

TIMELINE

1682 - René-Robert Cavelier de La Salle claims the Mississippi River valley for France.

1718 - New Orleans is founded at a bend in the Mississippi River.

1722 - New Orleans becomes the capital of Louisiana.

1762 - Spain assumes control of Louisiana in a treaty with France.

1788 - A fire destroys most of the buildings in New Orleans.

1800 - France regains control of Louisiana.

1803 - With the Louisiana Purchase, New Orleans becomes part of the United States.

1840 - New Orleans is the fourth-largest port in the world.

1965 - Hurricane Betsy hits New Orleans.

2005 - On August 29, Hurricane Katrina floods most of New Orleans.

EARLY HISTORY

Native Americans were the first people to live in present-day New Orleans. These tribes included the Muskogean, Caddo, and Tunica. They hunted and farmed along the Mississippi River.

In 1682, explorer René-Robert Cavelier de La Salle claimed the Mississippi River valley for France. He named it Louisiana after France's King Louis XIV. In 1698, King Louis sent Jean-Baptiste Le Moyne to colonize the area.

René-Robert Cavelier de La Salle

Native American guides led Le Moyne and his expedition inland along a trail. At a bend in the river, Le Moyne found the perfect place to establish a colony. In 1718, settlers began clearing the area for a new city. They also built **levees** to keep the city from flooding.

The new city was named Nouvelle-Orléans, or "New Orleans," after France's Duke of Orléans. In 1722, New Orleans became the capital of Louisiana. France controlled Louisiana until 1762. Then, King Louis XV signed it over to Spain in a secret treaty. However, the people of New Orleans continued to speak and live in the French ways.

New Orleans was nicknamed "Crescent City" because it was founded at a bend in the Mississippi River.

CONSTRUCTION

In 1788, a fire destroyed 856 of the city's 1,100 buildings. New Orleanians began rebuilding. However, another fire destroyed about 200 buildings six years later. After the second fire, city codes became more controlled. As structures were added or rebuilt, New Orleans started to have a more Spanish look.

Spain ruled the area for many years. Then in 1800, France regained control of Louisiana. Three years later, France sold the land as part of the Louisiana Purchase. This territory extended from the Mississippi River to the Rocky Mountains and from Canada to the Gulf of Mexico. The U.S. government paid $15 million for the land. With this sale, New Orleans became part of the United States.

At that time, most of New Orleans's residents were **Creole**. But in 1812, other **immigrants** began arriving in the city. They included German, French, and Irish people. Other Americans also moved to New Orleans. They all were attracted by the city's **economic** growth.

BATTLE OF NEW ORLEANS

From 1812 to 1814, the United States fought Great Britain in the War of 1812. During the war, U.S. general Andrew Jackson had many victories. On January 8, 1815, his army saved New Orleans from the British in the Battle of New Orleans.

The Battle of New Orleans was fought between more than 6,000 U.S. troops and 7,500 British troops. The United States won the battle after only 30 minutes. However, neither side was aware that the war had already ended when the Treaty of Ghent was signed in December 1814.

New Orleanians cheer for General Jackson as he parades through the city after his 1815 victory.

STEADY GROWTH

Over the next few years, New Orleans continued to grow. It soon became a major cotton port. Steamships entered the city by way of the Mississippi River. By 1840, New Orleans was the fourth-largest port in the world. That same year, its population reached 80,000.

After the **Civil War**, the city's population continued to increase, but its port activity declined. It wasn't until after **World War II** that New Orleans's **economy** began to recover.

In the 1950s, New Orleanians worked to improve the city. They built a new railroad terminal and widened the streets. Engineers also added height to the **levees**. Soon, new industries began entering the city, including oil **refineries**.

Then in 1965, Hurricane Betsy hit New Orleans. Flood waters topped the levees and caused major damage. After Betsy, the Army Corps of Engineers added to the levees again.

But, the city began to decline in the 1980s. The oil business started losing money. Many citizens were unemployed and housing was scarce.

Despite these problems, New Orleanians love their city. They are proud of their **culture** and welcome visitors from around the world. However, in 2005 New Orleanians were tested once again.

Steamboats greatly influenced the growth of the Port of New Orleans. In fact, the first steamboat ever to travel the Mississippi River was named the **New Orleans**.

KATRINA

On August 29, 2005, Hurricane Katrina hit the Gulf Coast. The storm claimed more than 1,000 lives. It also caused flooding in 80 percent of New Orleans.

Some people **evacuated** the area before the storm hit. However, those who were unable to leave were trapped without food, water, or electricity. For weeks, the Louisiana Superdome and the Ernest N. Morial Convention Center housed more than 10,000 people!

Many victims were taken to surrounding states and communities not affected by the hurricane. Three weeks later, Hurricane Rita caused even more flooding. Slowly, New Orleanians began to

U.S. president George W. Bush toured the area around the Louisiana Superdome in his helicopter, Marine One.

Hurricane Katrina had 145 mile per hour (233 km/h) winds. The winds and rain caused the city's levees to break in two places and Lake Pontchartrain to flood.

return to the city. They also started to rebuild the city and reinforce the 130 miles (209 km) of **levees**.

Katrina wasn't the first major hurricane to hit New Orleans. The city is 100 miles (161 km) north of where the Mississippi River flows into the Gulf of Mexico. So, hurricanes often threaten the area. Hurricane season is from June to November.

The city's climate is considered **semitropical**. From May to September, New Orleans is hot and **humid**. Winter occurs from December to March. However, New Orleans rarely has freezing temperatures. The city receives about 57 inches (145 cm) of rain a year.

SURROUNDED

The city of New Orleans covers 181 square miles (469 sq km) of land. However, the New Orleans Metropolitan Statistical Area (MSA) is much larger and contains several parishes, or **counties**. They are Jefferson, St. Bernard, St. Tammany, St. Charles, St. John the Baptist, Plaquemines, and Orleans parishes.

Lake Pontchartrain forms the northern border of New Orleans. Most of the city is located between the lake and the east bank of the Mississippi River. The section of the city known as Algiers is on the river's west bank.

Industrial Canal connects the Mississippi to Lake Pontchartrain to the north. And, the Mississippi River-Gulf Outlet links New Orleans with the Gulf of Mexico. This passage is 40 miles (64 km) shorter than the river route to the gulf.

New Orleans's location makes it an important U.S. port. The city exports grain, tobacco, oil, and other products. It is also a major manufacturing center. Food, clothing, and transportation equipment are all made in the city.

New Orleans has a long history and an important location. These qualities make it a great place to visit. The city's hotels and attractions provide jobs for New Orleanians. But many citizens are unemployed.

MISSISSIPPI

The Lake Pontchartrain Causeway is the world's longest bridge. It is 24 miles (39 km) long.

The Mississippi River influences New Orleans's transportation system. Barges, steamships, and trains carry cargo and people to and from the city. There are also two commercial airports near New Orleans. They are the Louis Armstrong New Orleans International Airport and the New Orleans Airport.

The Mississippi River divides New Orleans in half. The majority of the city is located on the east bank of the river. To cross the Mississippi, people take the Greater New Orleans or the Huey P. Long bridges. And, the Lake Pontchartrain Causeway connects the city to the north side of Lake Pontchartrain.

Many citizens drive cars across these bridges into downtown New Orleans. This often causes traffic jams and limited parking. So, buses and taxis also transport people downtown. There are two streetcar lines that help people get around the city as well.

Passengers take the Canal Street Ferry across the Mississippi River. The ferry carries people and vehicles between Algiers and the French Quarter.

ELECTION DAY

Mayor Ray Nagin

A mayor and a seven-member council govern New Orleans. They are all elected to four-year terms. New Orleans is divided into five political districts. Each district elects a council member. Two more at-large members are also on the council. These at-large officials represent the entire city, rather than a single district.

The mayor appoints a chief administrative officer. He or she prepares the annual budget for the city. The chief administrative officer also supervises the 14 city departments.

In May 2002, Mayor Ray Nagin was elected to office. He aimed to rid the city government of dishonest behavior. After Hurricane Katrina, Mayor Nagin began working to help citizens rebuild the city. He was re-elected in May 2006.

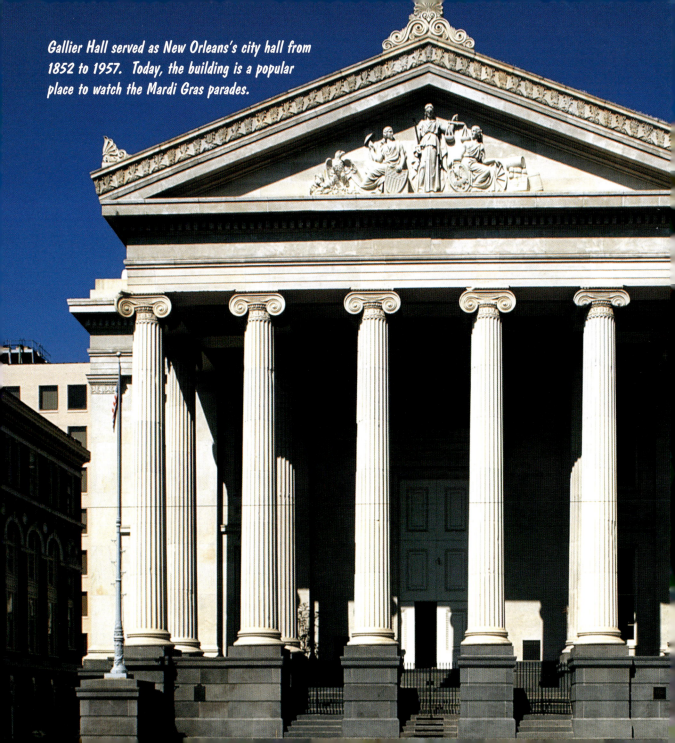

Gallier Hall served as New Orleans's city hall from 1852 to 1957. Today, the building is a popular place to watch the Mardi Gras parades.

NEW ORLEANIANS

    Hurricane Katrina caused many New Orleanians to leave town while the damage was repaired. But normally, 484,674 people call the city home. Two-thirds of this population is African American. Whites, Hispanics, Asians, and other small **ethnic** groups make up the rest of the population.

    New Orleans is separated into neighborhoods based on these different groups. One of the city's most recognized areas is the French Quarter. This is the oldest part of the city. There, **Creole** influence is evident in the **architecture**, food, and celebrations.

    Creole is also the name of one kind of local cooking. It is a highly seasoned combination of French and Spanish flavors. Common ingredients in Creole dishes include rice, **okra**, tomatoes, and peppers. Many citizens dine at restaurants to enjoy Creole and Cajun foods.

    Most New Orleanians rent apartments in the city or in one of the surrounding parishes. Only 40 percent own their homes. Unfortunately, more than one-quarter of the citizens live in poverty. And, housing is not available for many of these people. But, the city is working to improve housing conditions.

CAJUNS

The term Cajun comes from the word "Acadian." Acadians were people who came to Louisiana from Canada. The first Acadians arrived in the New Orleans area around 1765.

Despite the Creole influence in Louisiana, the Cajun culture has flourished. The distinctive features of this culture are seen most in New Orleans's cooking and music.

Cajun food is similar to Creole food, with gumbo, jambalaya, and crawfish pie as staple dishes. However, Cajun cooking is often spicier. This is due to the ample use of spices and peppers. In fact, Tabasco got its start in Cajun Country. Andouille, or Acadian smoked sausage, is often used in gumbo.

Cajun music is influenced by the Acadians' French heritage, as well as the heritage of the Creoles of African descent. Cajun music is easily recognized by its use of fiddles, accordions, and guitars. Its danceable folk songs are usually sung in Cajun French.

New Orleans chef Paul Prudhomme holds a skillet of jambalaya outside his Cajun restaurant. Jambalaya is seasoned rice usually cooked with ham, sausage, chicken, or shrimp.

The campus of Loyola University

Religion is important to many New Orleanians. Some people are **Protestant**. Others practice **voodoo**. However, most people in New Orleans are Roman Catholic. Early settlers brought this religion to the city. The annual Mardi Gras celebration is rooted in Catholic beliefs.

Catholicism has also influenced New Orleans's education system. There are many private Catholic schools in the city. There are also about 140 public schools in New Orleans. Louisiana requires children ages 7 to 17 to attend school.

A typical plantation home in New Orleans

There are also 13 colleges and universities in New Orleans. They include the University of New Orleans, Loyola University, and Tulane University. These institutions are some of the most respected schools in Louisiana.

English is the most common language in New Orleans. However, visitors to the city often expect to hear residents speaking in French or with a Southern drawl. Yet, the New Orleans accent is actually very similar to the East Coast accent.

THINGS TO SEE

Vieux Carré is French for "Old Square." It is also a name for the French Quarter. The French- and Spanish-style buildings give this area the look of a European city. The French Quarter contains Jackson Square and St. Louis Cathedral. These sights, as well as Bourbon Street, attract many tourists.

Celebrations also draw visitors to the city. Carnival begins on January 6 and ends with Mardi Gras. During these weeks, parades and decorative balls are held day and night. People often dress in costumes, crowns, and masks during the celebration. Mardi Gras, or "Fat Tuesday,"

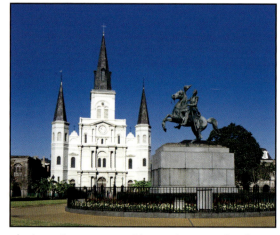

Jackson Square is a public garden named in honor of Andrew Jackson after his Battle of New Orleans victory. The statue in the center is General Jackson on a rearing horse. St. Louis Cathedral is the square's structural centerpiece.

Carnival was brought over from France and was most likely passed on through the centuries by the Creoles. The entire city of New Orleans is involved in this celebration. During Mardi Gras, the postal service even stops delivering mail!

is the day before Ash Wednesday. Afterward, the Catholic citizens observe Lent, a time of fasting.

New Orleans also has many year-round **cultural** attractions. They include the New Orleans Museum of Art, the New Orleans Historic **Voodoo** Museum, and the Aquarium of the Americas. New Orleanians also enjoy the theater, opera, and symphony.

THINGS TO DO

New Orleanians love music. Jazz especially is an important part of the city's culture. Many famous jazz musicians got their start there.

There are many other things to experience in New Orleans. Its citizens love music and dancing. The city is known as the birthplace of jazz. Every spring, it hosts the New Orleans Jazz and Heritage Festival.

People enjoy many outdoor activities in New Orleans, such as boat and cemetery tours. Many tourists also enjoy visiting City Park. It is the fifth-largest city park in the United States. It has sculpture gardens, a golf course, and a miniature theme park.

Horse racing, fishing, and many other sports are popular in New Orleans. The New Orleans Saints play football at the Louisiana Superdome. The New Orleans Hornets play basketball at the New Orleans Arena.

Whether working or playing, New Orleanians are friendly. They enjoy showing visitors their city. After the hurricane in 2005, citizens began working to make New Orleans once again a prosperous city and a popular travel destination.

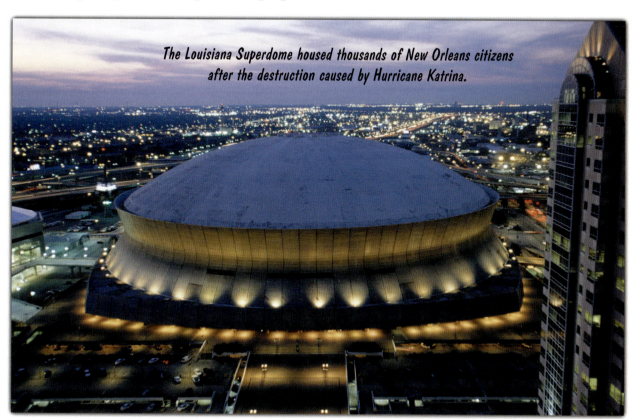

The Louisiana Superdome housed thousands of New Orleans citizens after the destruction caused by Hurricane Katrina.

GLOSSARY

architecture - the art of planning and designing buildings. A person who designs architecture is called an architect.
civil war - a war between groups in the same country. The United States of America and the Confederate States of America fought a civil war from 1861 to 1865.
county - the largest local government within a state of the United States.
Creole - a white person descended from early French or Spanish settlers. Also, a person of mixed French or Spanish and African descent.
culture - the customs, arts, and tools of a nation or people at a certain time.
economy - the way a nation uses its money, goods, and natural resources.
ethnic - of or having to do with a group of people who have the same race, nationality, or culture.
evacuate - to leave or be removed from a place, usually for protection.
humid - having moisture or dampness in the air.
immigrate - to enter another country to live. A person who immigrates is called an immigrant.
levee - a ridge of earth built along a river to prevent flooding.
okra - the pod of a plant that is used as flavoring in soup or stew.
Protestant - a Christian who does not belong to the Catholic Church.
refinery - the building and machinery used for purifying products such as sugar and petroleum.
semitropical - of, relating to, or being the regions bordering on the tropical zone.

voodoo - a set of mysterious religious rites characterized by a belief in sorcery and the power of charms. It originated in western Africa.

World War II - from 1939 to 1945, fought in Europe, Asia, and Africa. Great Britain, France, the United States, the Soviet Union, and their allies were on one side. Germany, Italy, Japan, and their allies were on the other side.

SAYING IT

Creole – KREE-ohl
Jean-Baptiste Le Moyne – zhahn-baw-teest luh mwawn
Mardi Gras – MAHR-dee grah
okra – OH-kruh
Pontchartrain – PAHN-chuhr-trayn
René-Robert Cavelier de La Salle – ruh-nay-raw-behr kaw-vuhl-yay duh law sawl

WEB SITES

To learn more about New Orleans, visit ABDO Publishing Company on the World Wide Web at **www.abdopublishing.com**. Web sites about New Orleans are featured on our Book Links page. These links are routinely monitored and updated to provide the most current information available.

INDEX

A
attractions 17, 22, 24, 26, 27, 28

B
Betsy (hurricane) 12

C
Canada 10
climate 15

E
economy 10, 12, 16, 17
education 24, 25

F
food 22
France 4, 8, 9, 10, 22, 26

G
Germany 10
government 20

H
housing 12, 22, 23

I
immigrants 10
Ireland 10

K
Katrina (hurricane) 4, 14, 15, 20, 29

L
La Salle, René-Robert Cavelier de 8
language 9, 25, 26
Le Moyne, Jean-Baptiste 8
Louis XIV (king of France) 8
Louis XV (king of France) 9
Louisiana Purchase 10

M
Mexico, Gulf of 4, 10, 14, 15, 16
Mississippi River 4, 8, 10, 12, 15, 16, 18

N
Nagin, Ray 20
Native Americans 8

O
Orléans, Duke of 9

P
Pontchartrain, Lake 4, 16, 18

R
religion 24, 27
Rita (hurricane) 14
Rocky Mountains 10

S
Spain 4, 9, 10, 22, 26
sports 29

T
transportation 12, 18, 19

W
wars 12

T 42875

42875

976.3　Hedlund, Stephanie F.,
Hed　　　New Orleans

BATTLE GROUND ACADEMY
Franklin, TN